FAYAN

THE STORM IN THE MIND

SANJAY V. YERNE

ISBN 979-888606263-2

The one who guides me forever

Translator

Prof. Haridas S. Fating. Sir

Thank you very much

Contents

storybook

THE STORM IN THE MIND

FAYAN

writter

Sanjay V. Yerne

Translator

Prof. Haridas S. Fating. Sir

FOREWORD

'Fyan' is my first collection of translated stories in English to be published. This story has come before the readers in Marathi language in the form of a collection of stories called 'Dufara'. The translation of these stories into English by Professor Haridas Fitting Sir has made it possible for my story to be made available to English readers and spread around the world. It is my duty to thank him for that.

With this collection of stories, I became famous all over Maharashtra. As a storyteller, I was more than happy to tell the story, but my heart was troubled by the sadness of the society, I was not allowed to sit still. From this, the writing of this story came to an end. This journey of storytelling is like a journey of my own life. I think so.

In the tough life journey of life, in every moment I have experienced the nature of the story. It was revealed through social thought. The realistic nature of social life, the unspoken acting of the personality in it, the compassion that pierces the heart, seems to be the emotional basis of family and social conscience. That's why I chose storytelling. The stories that come before the reader are not at all compromising with fiction. But these are sensitive stories that deliberately underline the philosophy of human thought and reality in society.

It seems to me that the reader should examine his mind, taking it to heart, rather than taking it head on. "Did you really enjoy it?" So through this story I have seen a weeping, speechless reader. I have cried a lot while telling this story. I have often experienced the sorrow of the society from my sorrow. My story was translated into English; the readers will decide how much it deserves translation as compared to the literary value. But one thing to say, the difficulty in translating the words in my dialect, the dialogue, was in fact a test for the translator. But the story comes to us in some way. This story is going to give a twist to the working soul. The common man will feel yours. Definitely would love to. It will be instructive, not just meaningful. From that new ideology will be sown in the society. This is a reasonable expectation.

The social awareness that comes from this story is important and instead of giving something to the reader, I am asking for the gift of something precious in life. That is all we need to understand. The meaning of the caste system, the differences in the society between the subject, misery, misery, poverty, the hoopla of women and how the mind of goodness should be realized by a storyteller. Through this, I have been able to unravel the emotional turmoil of the mind. Although the subject is simple, the story brings you new hope, new concept, new subject. The characters, dialogues, events and happenings in each story are giving you something. That's all there is to it. This is my story for the sake of humanity in this world.

I look forward to hearing from you. There will be some shortcomings in it; I will not deny it on the test of linguistics. The purpose behind this is to convey to you the translation done by Professor Fating Sir. This story comes to us through the publication of 'Pencil'. In this collection, I am also thankful to Sir Durvekant Bankar for his proofreading using his language skills. It is my duty to thank all my readers and literary friends for this purpose. My wife Mrs. This is why we come across books in the form of books, which help in the creation of music, children Parth, Shiva, Kavya. I would like to thank all the friends for their direct and indirect cooperation.

When the story is translated and presented, you will be interested. I feel that the changing lifestyle, our mind, our aspirations will transform this story into a banyan tree.

Sanjay V. Yerne
Nagbhid, Dist- Chandrapur.
Mo. 9404121098

PREFACE

"Fayan" a collection of ten stories is being presented by Mr. Sanjay Yerne sir. It imparts me an immense joy to have this book in English language.

Fyan is a name given to the storm, which struck the Konkan coast in 2009. The storm didn't do it. The thrilling experience experienced by the citizens, however, the fear in the mind is always haunted by such a storm. Even today, the world of many who were caught in the storm has not stood still. The story of Fyan is a parody of the role of the government. Ten such stories are included in this collection. The author expects that the stories which create a storm of innumerable thoughts in the mind, will change the thoughts and feelings in our hearts and inculcate a human value. That is why this collection is named Fyan.

English language is called as the window of the world. All the knowledge -may be technical, technological, moral, medical, spatial, geological is inserted in English language. As it is our international language, our general lives may be covered with it. Our kids or students may rich in the spoken and psychological understanding of this language. As per these norms, Mr. Sanjay Yerne sir has been done a very good job by presenting this collection of stories.

Though all these stories are imaginary but the real reflection of rural life and the language used in it is very highly appreciable and countable. 'Dafara, sevawrati, Balloons of hair' are the stories which have a full sense of rural touch and dialect. The occasions are picturized with a great sensibility which has the ability to respond a complex emotional or aesthetic influences.

Mr. Sanjay Yerne sir is not a debutant author but a fully cogitable and congnisable. He has a curiosity to present the special events before the people to have a moderate modification between them. This literature is also one of the intrinsic actification done by him.

'Fayan, Difference, Sonzari, Surkuda, Inda' are same stories included in this book. 'Sonzari' is the story in which the reflection of immense poverty is to be shown. This is the community which collects the gold. iron or metal particles from the ashes. What a terrible prospect it is! 'Surkuda' is the story of farmer who died due to the acute poverty but having a push to educate his kids.

So the most achievable and clear depicted stories are suggested to the people. It is remarkable better try by Mr. Sanjay Yerne Sir.

I hope that this book will surely enable the students as well as people for the sake of their English knowledge. It will definitely boost the confidence level of the readers.

"Education is a social process for the reconstructions of the society." - John Dewey.

Again finally I hope that this book will receive a warm welcome from the people and deploy to enhance the educational energy among the people.

With warm wishes.

Durvekant T. Bankar
English expertteacher
Bramhapuri.

I

Dafara

'Dumdum' beating of the 'Dafara' was heard in the month of Chaitra. "The scorching of the sun and beating drum" was great fun of dancing on the beat of Dafara In the fair of Salubai. We all the children of cobblers used to wait for that occasion.

We thought the fair of Salubai will bring a new wave of fun as we were learning and reading some books. My mother waved her palm on my forehead and blessed me. I would be spared from the evil eye.

We use to earn our bread and butter from the month of the Chaitra by beating the Dafara's when we had no farm work. I was also able to give heat of Fire to the Dafara and Beat It. I used to see a movement of beating from my father and I learned how to beat the Dafara.

After the Vaishakh month, my father used to beat the Dafara and earn something. I used to tie Ghungur do ankles and walk behind my father. In the bridegroom's marriage procession, some drunkards used to dance and cast some money. I would collect it. Patil of the village would keep a rupee note of the ground as a gift and my father would lift that not jumping down, sticking the note to the forehead while beating the Dafara and dancing. People would feel joy. I used to keep that note in the pocket of my torn pant. After the procession I would ask father, "Ba, will you buy me a new pair of pants?"

Ba would gladly say, 'yes'. I would run after him hoping for getting a new pant.

Sometimes some rich people would give Ba a Dhoti, a long cloth to wear, and a blouse to mother as a gift in marriage. Nowadays people are becoming miser for giving gifts in the marriage for beating the Dafara. They would spend a lot of money on drinking.

Ba would say that we have been staying on the outskirts of the village Shankarpur since my birth. My family had to wander from village to village and would stay for four-five days in a village to keep both ends meet. Such was our Vagrant life. We had the company of two dogs, four-five pigs, and one ass carrying belongings, and the Dafara for beating for livelihood in life.

Our main profession was to take out skin from the carcass of the dead animals. We waited for the death of the animal. As soon as an animal was found dead, we assembled there to take out its skin. We were accompanied by dogs, vultures, and flies that were there for eating flesh. After four-five days, a skeleton remained there and we used to sell the bones of the animal for ten paisa kilogram. While cleaning the dirt in the society, nobody came near us and we used to stay away from society. We were considered untouchables and of below-dignity people. But when they had the celebrations of wedding, nomination, engagement, or death, they had to depend on us for the beating of our Dafara. We were very glad to see that. We used to get tasty meals otherwise we were fed on Varan-Bhat, Besan Bhakar, etc.

Shankarpur was somewhat a good village. We had our mud house built of mud and bamboos. People used to call us for any function. Mother used to go for fieldwork. I was the only child in a family to go to school. I was influenced by the saying of, Dr. Babasaheb, "Learn, unite and struggle." I was like a cub of a tiger at the beginning. I hesitated to go to school. Ba would advise me to learn to improve life. He would beat me also. I thought it was better to go to school.

Ba bought me a slate and pencil and took me to the school. Seeing my torn underwear and dirty shirt, all the students laughed. As I was a cobbler's son, nobody would allow me to sit beside him. **B**ut the teacher loved. He patted me and encouraged me to study. A big photograph of Babasaheb was in the classroom. On his birth anniversary, I was asked to garland the photograph of Babasaheb. I would observe the photograph and liked to become like Babasaheb. Year after year, I passed and now passed the seventh class board exam.

Ba came to school on that day. A teacher asked him to serve sweets like pedas. Ba became extremely glad, Went to the shop and bought some pedas; gave one to the teacher. I touch the feet of the teacher and the photograph of Babasaheb with gratitude. Our eyes were filled with tears.

"Aare, my cub passed the exam and now he will become Saheb. Goddess Salubai blessed us." Ba said, He told everybody proudly. Mother was also very glad. Her Joys had no bounds.

The fair of goddess Salubai was after four days. Our small vagrant families of cobblers used to assemble in the fair on the night of Chitra. We lit the firewood, worshipped the Goddess, beat the Dafaras, and dance together. Marriages were arranged people would drink and eat chicken or mutton and celebrate. My sister Rama's marriage was arranged Shankarya. He was educated equally to me. My parents were very glad and arrange a dinner party in the name of the Goddess. Our relatives drank but Ba did not touch liquor. Ba had given up drinking for twelve years.

Ba used to advise others, "Listen to Babasaheb, We should give up old traditions. We leave to change our Lifestyle. We will have to be away from slavery told by Mahatma Phule. People feeding milk to snacks do not give even water to others. Tukaram Maharaj used to say to abolishing evils is also non-violence. A man who takes us near is our God. Buddha, Shivba, Mahatma Phule, Shahu Maharaj, Babasaheb, Punjabrao, Periyar Swami, etc. took labor to change the lifestyle and thinking of others."

Ba was uneducated but they had respect in our society. Now I was fifteen years old. Others suggested Ba arrange my marriage. Ba refused them saying that I would become an officer build a house in a city and then would get married.

After the four days fair, all the families were leaving for their villages embracing each other.

We had the only work of beating Dafaras in the summer in the marriage or death rituals- in the marriage ceremony of Patil's Son, We beat Dafaras for four days. He gave clothes to all as a gift. Ba sewed a shirt and pants for me from a tailor. We had to go to dinner with our plates and glasses. After dinner, we used to collect left food from others' plates and bring it home. It would last for four-five days as it was driest in the sun.

Now I was grown up and educated. I delivered a lecture at the Republic Day function and people clapped. I was clever in the class and the students respected me.

Rama's marriage was coming nearer to be held in the month of Jeshtha. All the relatives assembled. The groom Shankarya came with his relatives to get married to Rama. Tamarind was applied to Rama was made bride in new clothes. The next day the photograph of Babasaheb was garlanded and Rama got married to Shankar. She went to her husband's village in a procession. The Dafara was being beaten in front of the procession. I was looking at standing under the Tamarind tree. My eyes were full of tears to see my only sister leaving us and going to her husband's house.

Ba called me, "O dear lad, Patil's Mother died. They have called us. Go and bit the Dafara in the death procession." I took the photograph of Babasaheb and kept it inside my home. I looked at the suit dress of Babasaheb in the photograph. I had the challenge to become like Babasaheb.

I took the Dafara and beating stick. I was walking ahead of the dead bodies, last procession and was beating the Dafara in the rhythm of "Dhenganag Dheng... khuchalang kuchalang.....sssss." The dead body was kept on a pyre and was burned. The flame of fire was raising high and high. I was thinking of Babasaheb to become great. I was beating the Dafara very loudly for the last time. And all of sudden I threw the Dafara and stick in the fire never to beat. All were looking at me curiously. I was walking ahead of all.....

II

Sevawrati

When I parked the car in the college, I came to know. Today is the death anniversary of saint Gadge Baba. Yes, I had forgotten it. I had been out of college and busy with other works, I did not know it. My heart was overwhelmed.

The student had made vast and fast preparations for the program in the hall. If observed, it is common that the birth and death anniversary of a great person and other programs to motivate students are organized in colleges.Our college earned a reputation in this field and so the student and staff member like and favor the college.

I have been serving in my college for the last ten years. As soon as I had cleared the net, Ph.D., I was appointed as a professor in the college. The reason was that the founder of the education society of our college was of the thinking of Saint Gadge Baba or the great men of the Bahujan thoughts. His honest personality was a great Legacy to the student.

The program started. The orators, the founder of the society, and other reputed persons were on the dais. My mind was overwhelmed as I look at the photograph of Saint Gadge Baba. Prof. Manmode in his impressive and thought-provoking speech said on God, fortune sin and sinlessness, Vaidik Manuwadi life and how to overcome upon them.

"Don't be a stone; find a real man in stone instead of God. Behave like a man. Find God in man. Don't rob the helpless. Our Bahujan Samaj is leading a life in the slavery of the cultural and social conflict and we have no idea of it. We should think of it logically. If we Bahujan people think understand and follow the thoughts of Saint Gadge Baba, our life will be glittering like gold on the earth. Our thoughts have been given brakes and speed is stopped. Be prepared to abolish the fake thoughts! Jagadguru Tukobaray says, "We will devote our underwear to a polite friend, otherwise beat a stick on the head of the foe!" It is the religion and work of manliness."

Students clapped hands. I begin to dream of the optimistic life of the new generations of the student while looking at the photograph of Saint Gadge Baba. I had no attention on clapping also; I would deliver lectures on a dais. Today, I was not the chief guest nor I had delivered a lecture in my college. Mercy a listener. I was observing the selfless photograph of Saint Gadge Baba as if Baba standing before me and I was embarrassing him. I was imagining, he was gathering me in his arms and I was weeping. I was remembering my past life poverty and conflicts.

I had a fact made of mud, rough scrap papers, and olden tin shed. Mother, younger Pamya, and I used to live in that small shed near the railway iron bridge. Some ten to twelve homeless people like us encroached on the sites near us and they were preparing their mud huts. During the rainy season, the huts were full of filtering rainwater and nearby were dump of Thrown garbage. The dirty smell of the degrading garbage made civilized people unable to pass by the road but it was our destiny to live in that area. It was an open area used for the open latrine. We were used to that dirty smell and dirty area and we had to live by fate in that area. Any way mother used to earn and bring us up.

I had an understanding. When I was in the seven-eight standard. I used to learn in municipality School. Mother admitted me there. She used to work as a maidservant in the owner of the mill and feed us. Father expired in our childhood. He was a drunkard and earned nothing, a real problem to mother. One day, he drank too much and died wanting water. Mother said that "She was free from the tyranny of drunkard husband." "Kapalache Kunku Gele Pan bes Jhale." Father used to quarrel and beat mother. They were living in a village, after that came to the city with other identities, raised a mud teen shade near this Railway iron Bridge.

The local railway train used to cross the iron bridge making a loud sound. Its sound of while and the harsh sound of passing wheels used to encourage me. After observing the playing train four-five times a day, my mind used to leap and run like it. I didn't know what its relations were with me.

It was nighttime at about ten A.M. After passing the Last Local train now, the iron bridge and the area will be calm thoughts out the night like me. We all people living in the hutments used to sleep under the iron bridge. Some vagrant dwellers used to come and sleep there. The slum area was our world. Whom will we tell our sorrows and who will hear? My mother used to tell me to become like the children of the rich. She used to hope that our days would also change. I would tell her that I would become so. She used to say 'Definitely you will be learned like Babasaheb."

Mother's words encouraged me. I would study in the street light sitting under the iron bridge. All the children in the slum used to come and watch me. Most of the children use to collect scraps like plastic bags, bottles, iron pieces, etc., and earn something. My mother never asked used to collect those abandoned things.

My mother called me, "come to take supper, all slept and you are studying, now the local will arrive, eat something and then study."

The local train departed making a 'Dhadalak dhad...dhad' sound. I rubbed my palms to my pant and began to eat. Mother asked, "Is there an exam ahead now? Will you pass the exam this year also?"

"Not only me but anybody can pass in the exam. But I have to achieve the first number in the class," I said.

"Do children like ours get the first number?" Marks are given on seeing the face of the rich."

She said, "Officers' children do get the numbers."

"No, mother, it is not so. He is clever and attending the tuition classes also."

"So you are not clever?"

"It is not so, one has to study hard to a achieve good grade."

"Do do something good, become great, I am tired of living of this slum living. But we can do nothing also," she said.

"We have got the place to live in also good for us. Some are wandering from place to place. It is heard that some minister promised the slum dwellers to allot the constructed houses," I said. She was satisfied.

"Where did you bring this tasty food from?" I asked.

"Pamya had gone to hold the lights poles in the marriage procession. He brought the food in cloth."

All the dwellers were sleeping under the bridge. My kerosene lamp was still burning dimly. I was tired of reading. Mother slept in the hut. I went inside the hut, drank a glass of water, and came to sleep under the bridge. The stars were shining as if encouraging me.

All the streets were deserted. I took an older, torn bed sheet, covered it on my body, and slept. In the meantime, a car from a deserted street came and stopped near the bridge. A tall man came out of the car; He opened the back door of the car, took some bundles and came to us. I was looking at what he was to do. I woke and sat. All slept.

I asked him "Who he was."

"I have brought, you some gifts"

"What gifts?" I asked

"Some blankets, bed sheets. You are all sleeping in the open place. I see you are shivering from the cold. I am giving you those small gifts as social service. Today is the death anniversary of Saint Gadge Baba.

He covered the blankets on all the sleeping people, gave them on to Pamya also. I was looking at him and saw God in him then he came to me and gave me one blanket, a bed sheet. I was observing his bright, glad face of satisfaction. He went to his car. I went too but his car left soon. I could not say even thanks to that Godman.

By hearing the sound of clapping, I came to the attention, the speech was over. The guest was coming down from the dais. A vote of thanks was given. I was mingled in the thoughts of my childhood. I was staring at the idol of selfless Saint Gadge Baba. I saluted him in mind. Students got everything on how to lead a life in the speeches.

I returned home in the noon. My mood was good. Mrs. was ready to go shopping. The photographs of Bahujan Samaj great persons Jijau, Gadge Baba, etc. were hung on the walls. I garlanded them and prayed Jijau Vandana. My little daughter Shreya said, "Papa, I want jeans pants, and flowers top." I took them to the Marketplace.

We spent an hour for shopping. We bought clothes after a good observation. While observing the clothes, I remembered my past life in a hut in that slum. I became a professional by studying wearing form and olden clothes, studying in a dom-lit kerosene lamp. Younger brother Pramod also became an engineer. Mother is not alive. I got to the job and she had paralyzed stroke. She could not live in her son's new home. Her dreams of living in the new home reminded unfulfilled.

Often I was remembering my mother. The salary of the first month of service was kept on her foot. She left his world after four days. I was weeping in her memory. Then I got married. She could not see her daughter-in-law. Pramod also got married and did a job in the city. If mother was alive, she would have survived for five-six years more. Dedicating her life to us, she left this world. She was a fairy to us.

"Take this bill, please, all shopping is done." heard the voice of Mrs. and I come to attention. I paid the bill. I bought two dresses for myself, Mrs. brought two sarees, and my daughter brought pants, a top, and other necessities.

After taking snacks a stall was going ahead on foot. We heard the sound of speeches on a dais at the next square. We went there. A program was arranged there in memory of the death anniversary of Saint Gadge Baba. It was a crowded program. Speeches were going on the dais.

"Gadge Baba's work is so inspiring that everyone should take an oath to dedicate him for social service. Apart from the work village cleanliness, one should donate a cloth yearly to the needy," People should behave, "Je ka Ranjale Ganjale! Tyasi Mhane Jo aapule." the saying of Saint Tukaram Maharaj. I have been serving the needy by donating as per my capacity. Everyone should do such social work and it will be a real tribute to Saint Gadge Baba." the speech ended.

I was staring at the face of the orator. I thought I had seen him somewhere. He was distributing the clothes in the program. The needy, poor, helpless, the beggars. All crowded around him for helpless. I thought as if Gadge baba distributing the goods.

I look at the photograph of Gadge Baba on a dais. I thought as if Baba was calling me. We went there and touched the feet of Baba in the photograph. I know the face of the distributor. I took the bags of clothes from my wife's hand and handed them over to the distributor.

"Sir, these are clothes by me to distribute to the needy," I said.

He was staring at me. Tears rolled down from my eyes. I touched his feet and he accepted my gift to distribute. He took me in his arms and all were looking at me.

"Sir, your gifted blanket in my childhood is still giving me warm," I said.

My wife and daughters Shreya touched his feet. I was looking at the photograph of Gadge Baba and the face of that personality on the dais. I was remembering those childhood days under the iron bridge a person coming out of the car, his gifts of blankets and bed sheets and those days of poverty, etc. all were calling me, encouraging me to become a "Sevawrati."

III
Vihar

(religious Discussion House)

Baba used to meditate Trisharan under the large Bodhiwruksha. I used to go to the college in a taluka by bicycle crossing the distance of ten kilometers. It was my daily routine and used to return home in the evening. I have been working hard on the regular study and traveling from my high school education to P.G. classes. It was necessary for me to cross the Neema River. A hill near it and rough path daily.

Our village is small having about fifty huts and houses. Everybody depended on fieldwork. Some four-five boys were matriculated and none was collegiate. except me.

The Neema River was flowing in curve and there was a hill on the zig-zag path and there was a calm deserted Vihar on the hill covered with natural beauty that was consoling me. Nobody would have visited that deserted Vihar in solace this generation. But while walking by the side, I used to pray it in mind. I thought I would be blessed for fulfilling my future dreams. After the exam of the last year, I would have to search for a job.

Whenever I had spare time, I used to visit that Vihar. Its serenity, trees, river, etc. all were fascinating. Once I had taken my friend there for a picnic. They were very glad to visit it. But that time 'Baba' was not meditating Trisharan.

Today I was feeling weary. I had not gone to Vihar for three months. I took a bicycle and went to Vihar early in the morning crossing five kilometers distance.

Baba was sitting in meditations in the early morning under that Pipal tree. After meditation, he had attention on me. Going near, I was about to touch his feet. But he lifted my hands and said, "No, let it."

"But baba, I wish for your blessing."

"Aare, what blessing. I am a man like you?"

He took me near the trunk of Pipal tree. We sat there.

"Boy, where do you belong to?"

"Baba, I am from the neighboring village."

"Why did you come here in the early morning?"

"For a long time, I had not come here. While going to college every day, this Vihar was at if keep calling me. I thought I had some relations with it and nature."

"Baba, would I ask you one thing?"

"Yes, ask, boy, don't hesitate."

"How long have you been staying alone at such a deserted place and for what?"

"Aare, I am not alone here. You are here and you see this place is not deserted. Here, Lord Buddha…. all is fascinating me also."

Baba was talking about the holy secret. He drank Neema river water stored in a copper pot and gave me also. I told him everything about myself and my education aim. The sun was shining brightly. I took his permission and began to go to my village. He gave me a Pipal leaves as a present. I observed it. I kept it in my pocket. I was very glad.

Many days passed. I had got a part-time job in a city. I was settled there. I had no cares. I decided to take my parent to a city to live with me. I started to come to my village. I came near the Neema river, a curve path, and ancient deserted Vihar on the hill. I remembered that old Baba. I went near that Pipal tree. But Baba was not there. I was depressed. I sat under that people tree thinking of Baba. I sensed that nobody was living there. Wild grass was grown up everywhere. I left the place for my village.

Where would have Baba gone? Who he would be? Meditating Trisharan would be some great Mahant receiving supreme position and joy in life. That Vihar would have been constructed in the tenure of Ashoka-The great.

I reached my village after many days. As earlier suggested, my parents had made all the preparation to go city. I met everybody. I was sad to leave my native village and glad to settle in the city. I had mixed feelings in my mind. At night I had asked my mother about that Baba in the Vihar. She said he lived there for many days later nobody knew where he had gone. She said that Baba used to come to the village to beg for food daily. Without taking anything to anybody, he used to go back. But he was chanting Trisharan 'buddham... Saranam... gacchami.'

I have left my village for five years. I had a good job, father, mother, and wife also in the city. I was fully satisfied. Occasionally, I used to remember that village life, Neema River, hill, deserted Vihar and Baba. I was very eager to know about Baba.

I sat on a sofa reading a newspaper. I was reading the headline "staunch religious leader expired, Tribute to his preaching, thinking salute, Salam, JayBhim, etc. words were used.

We kill our people only for our willful thinking of religion. All leaves are green and any blood is red. But in the advent of science, all leaves are of different colors and in the future, the colors of blood would be changed. Man's religion would be identified in his colors of blood.

A staunch follower of the principles of lord Buddha our Baba living in the deserted on the hill took last breath and left heaven. My eyes were full of tears for Baba, who dedicated his whole life to spreading the principles of Lord Buddha and fulfilling the dreams of Babasaheb.

In a moment, I cried in mind Baba.... Yes, he was the same Baba who was chanting Trisharan all the time 'Budhham.... Saranam... Gacchami.' I was observing his photo and a special news bulletin in the newspaper.

My wife and I went to have the last look and pay homage to Baba. After many years, I was going by the over village path. We crossed the river Neema. That hills and reached the deserted Vihar.... Thousands of people assembled there for the cremation. Baba's dead body was kept under the Pipal tree in a sitting position seeing Buddha like face. I kept my head on his legs and began to weep. "My Baba..." Who talked me only once, had gone. The soft wind was blowing. A Pipal leaf fell from the tree and was flying towards the flow of the Neema River. The sweet chanting of Trisharan.....

"Buddham... Sharanam... Gachhami.

Dhammam... Sharanam Gachhami.

Sangham... Sharanam... Gacchami......"

IV

Balloons for Hair

Due to completions of many works. I slept late at night and woke up late at eight a.m. in the morning at the noise of shouting of selling something "Buy the Balloons.... Buy the balloons..."

Mashing eyes, I woke up and looked through the window. A woman of a slim figure is carrying her about one and half year child in torn cloth, having a basket of utensils on the head and was walking shouting, "Buy The balloons... Buy the balloons for hair." along the narrow lanes.

"Stop, come here." My wife Mathura called the woman from the door. The woman responded and kept her basket below and her child also.

"Tell mam, how much hair is available?"

"Take, those are enough, take them"

"You will get a pot worth ten rupees hair."

"Only pot... will not get somewhat a bigger thing?"

"Mam, what will be worth of last, damaged hair on head? Won't you throw them away? But they are used nowadays, so we buy them. We earn something by that."

"Well, give one some fine pot."

"Yes,"

I washed my eyes with cold water. I have had a habit of bed tea from my college life. I asked my wife for tea and began to read the headlines of news in the newspaper.

Today is the birthday of Mrs. Indira Gandhi, Who made the slogan "Remove Poverty."

Turning off the pages, I began to observe other news also and asked my wife "Is the tea prepared?"

"Yes, wait, it is being boiled on the stove."

Look! my hair is dispersing despite applying hair oil worth a hundred rupees a month and gets only ten rupees for selling that dispersed collected hair. It's also profit, isn't it?

She was talking likewise; I was observing the pot and that woman sitting in front of the door with her child. The women in neighborhood assembled around the woman. My wife, Mathura gave me a cup of tea. While drinking tea, I began to read the news. I looked at that loving slim blackish child in rugs' underwear. It looked like suffering from malt nutrition's, showing an exact picture of poverty.

I looked at that slim hawkish innocent woman wearing a mud-dish torn saree showing her poverty. I was overwhelmed. She was wandering from door to door to selling balloons to earn both ends meal.

She asked my wife if she could get some tea. She set out in the early morning, my wife was her first customer.

I felt pity for her. I was ashamed of myself for taking tea in front of that woman. I asked my wife to give her tea. In the meantime, she gave her tea. My wife would have felt pity for her. She also brought a glass of milk and a plate of bread and biscuits for her child.

"Why did you give so much?" She said,

"Your child would have been hungry." said, my wife.

I was going through the T.V. news. She was feeding her child. I was overwhelmed looking at the woman and her child. Poverty compels man to do anything. She was wandering from a place selling balloons to earn livelihood and feed her children.

Look at my wife; she has to do nothing at home. She has a maidservant to do house chores. It is better that she knows about poverty and everything else. Otherwise, she would not have helped others.

I came to the door and asked her, "What is the name of your village?"

"Kanapa."

"I mean, you belong to the Korku community."

"Yes, yes."

I asked her, "Can you run your house by selling balloons?"

"What should we do Saheb to feed the stomach? Doctor's in cities buy hair to make head wigs. We get some money for livelihood."

"What does your husband do?"

"He also does some work if gets. He earns something in the daytime and drinks too much at night and sleeps. If asked about it, he scolds me. What should I tell you more Saheb?"

She lifted her child on one side of her body and began to walk. She was smashing the balloon for a rough sound and shouting. "Take balloons for waste hair."

What a pathetic Lifestyle! I was thinking about the difference between the lifestyle of my Mathura and that woman. I could not enjoy the taste of lunch that day.

I went to the office. Today the function of the birth anniversary of Indira Gandhi was to be performed in a grand way and so all the preparations were made under the guidance of the ex-minister.

The chief guest and the dignitaries were on the dais. Employees like us were sitting in front. The program started with clapping hands.

The ex-home Minister began to speak "India's first woman Prime Minister, respect given to women, honor, the progress of women, the world is changing our country after sixty years of independence, etc. But I was remembering the figure and life of that balloon-selling woman to earn a livelihood. He concluded his speech saying. "We pay tribute to first woman Prime Minister Who gave the slogan of "Remove Poverty" and tiered to remove it in India. Jay Hind."

Many others spoke on our development schemes and planning, our honesty, the welfare of common people rainwater harvesting and I was the witness of how we are working or deceiving others. I was ashamed of myself.

Lastly, I was called to conclude the program. I proposed a vote of thanks But I had the same remembrance of that poor woman.

I said, "thanks to the ex-Home Minister for giving time for the program. I asked whether the slogan of Priyadarshani Indira Gandhi is being successful today. I think all the common people leading the life of poverty will one day commit suicide collectively because of the exploitation by the corrupt reach governing people and government nutrition and then nobody will be poor and the poverty will be removed. So who will work sincerely for the betterment of the common people and implement the slogan of Indiraji?

All the assembled audience responded to my speech with clapping hands. I saw the same balloon-selling woman carrying her child on one side of her body and listening to the speech. She was observing the banner of the program and the photograph of Indiraji. Her crying child, smashing rough sound of balloons,

Her shouting, "Take balloon.... take balloons for hair." all was awakening.....?

● 21 ●

V
Fayan

I was fully tired of daily routine work in the office. Common people would not get justice because of the modern tendency of employees of taking a commission for passing pending cases,

That old helpless grandmother today also came in office for taking compensation for the drought-hit crop. I could not tell when her work will be done. Her rugged saree and blouse reminded me of my mother. I gave her tea bought by the peon. All first she hesitated and then drank.

"Grandma, I know your trouble but what can I do? Next month you will not have to go empty-handed."

"Surely? My legs are aching; I would not survive long. There would be no need to come here if I had children. You are very good. The former officer was very rough by nature. God will bless you!"

She began to go back taking the support of her walking stick. I was looking at her somewhat sadly.

I turned on the T.V. at home and began to look at the news. Parth came home from school. Kissing him, I asked him about his study. My wife handed me a cup of tea.

The big breaking news was "The storm lashed, Fayan raged." Havoc was everywhere. All the T.V. news channels were telecasting the impact of Fayan on the seashore and destroying normal life.

The news was repeated showing all photography of the destructions. "More than a hundred fishermen missing in the sea. The ragging storm is becoming silent. Rising tides are making lifestyles smaller. Our reporter Kunal and the cameraman are giving news from the spot.

"Kunal, what is the situation there, how long you have been there? What is the role of the Government?"

"Neha, Fayan is the name of the storm. I arrived here by the speed of two-three hundred kilometers per hour at mid-day it reached rising the high tides in the sea. Coastal life is disturbed, scattered. Many fishermen are still missing. I reached her before the storm broke out. I was waiting for Fayan to have clear scenes. Neha, these are real pictures. Fayan turn down the boat flowing all fishermen in it. Who is responsible for this calamity? I will be visiting family members. It is difficult to calculate the protections and help to the victims. kunal with cameraman Ashu, speaking on Fayan from Kokan.... Neha."

It was surprising to see a reporter present on the spot before the storm. I was thinking calmly, turned off the T.V., and slept.

I received the phone from the office in the morning. The secretary was to visit the Fayan affected place along with office staff. I set out with our employees on the tour. Crossing the distance of about a hundred kilometers is despite weariness, we eagerly reached there the secretary along with the four-five vehicles reached there and observed the situation of destruction. Many disaster victims mate the site Saheb for help.

"Saheb, I have lost all the crops. How will I feed my four children, everything is gone Saheb." One man was telling and I could not see his Sorrows.

"Okay, we will help you in all ways. I talk to the seniors today. But despite the information of the arrival of Fayan, water will enter and affects the crop in fields, why didn't you cut the crops?" Saheb asked reversely.

That farmer wiping his tears with muddy Dupatta was staring at the Saheb. I suppressed my laugh. The reporter and cameraman were busy analyzing and taking photographs.

I reached home at night. Turning on the T.V. sat for dinner, I changed the news channels frequently but there was no news report of visit on any channel.

I began to guess the survey of the visit. I felt pity for my happy life. Before the rice crop was ready for harvesting, how will the farmers reap it before the rain? I was shocked and felt pity for the ignorance of the Saheb.

After dinner, I was laughing at myself like mad. Parth told this to his mom and I came to consciousness.

Many days passed. I had forgotten the impact of the Fayan. The public elections were declared and the code of conduct was in force. The canvassing was in full swing.

I went to the market to bring vegetables. My son also came with me. There was an elections rally. An ex-Minister was giving a lecture on rising prices, unemployment, farmer's problem, corruption, justice, morality, etc. I was standing hearing it at the backside. My son urged me to go home.

"Aare, those who do not have the knowledge farming, how can they give justice to the farmers? I am telling you the real story told by a farmer. "A Saheb, the officer was passing the road by the side of the farm. He stopped his car near it. The farmer watering his farm. The officer asked him, "What is this plant of?"

"It is a chilly plant," he said.

"It is a chilly plant? But chilly is red color. It is planted her of green color. Very good. We like it very much. I appreciate your research."

Saheb instantly asked his P.A. two asked the name of the farmer and forward his nomination for the 'Rashtriya Krishi Ratna Puraskar' Saheb went with stop and the farmer was watching him for his ignorance.

Everybody laughed with clapping hands. The party was cheered up. "Those who do not know the difference between green chili and it become red after drying......"

I begin to go home with Parth. At night, I was thinking about the speech and begin to laugh. I was also thinking about the destruction caused by Fayan. My wife asked me if I was not feeling well.

"No, No, I am well," I said,

Parth was asleep, thinking not to make wife sad, I took her hand in my hand, stared at her eyes, and asked "Does cotton rise in the bud is Flower?"

She was looking dumb staring at me only. Tears rolled down from my eyes. My wife felt it like Fayan. She embraced me taking me in her womb and began to shed tears.

I wiped off the tears. I heard the noise of that helpless old woman begging at our door, "Daughter, will you please give me some "Bhakar Bhaji?"

I came to consciousness and looked through the window.

I heard her voice again. My wife took about remaining 'Bhat and bhaji.' from the freeze and whet to give that woman.

I was looking at the back figure of the woman who was going out. The shining stars crowded in the sky. a soft breeze was blowing. I was thinking of Fayan. I fell on the bed covering a blanket on my body. I slept thinking as if I was found in a dream Fayan. T.V. was still on.................

VI
Difference

After reading the nameplate at the door, she came in smiling. Her face looked fresh as if of the rising tides in the sea.

"Aunty, I have to get the clothes sewed. May I come in?"

"Yes, come in."

She sat on the sofa putting three Salwar clothes on the table.

"Salwars are to be sewed? of what type?"

"One narrow, one three-phase, and one simple."

"Very good. How much cost it?"

"Not too much costly. Three for thousand rupees."

I took the size of her body. She was laughing.

"You are looking very glad."

"Of course, aunty, because I bought the dress after three years."

She was learning in the twelfth class.

"What is your name?"

"Uma Salve."

"Yes, come after fifteen days."

"No, aunty, I need at least one dress on tomorrow."

"No, there is a rush for sewing dresses and I cannot sew one urgently."

"No aunty, my math papers is on tomorrow and I think I must wear a new dress on the occasion."

The smile was disappearing on her face and she looked as if crying. "Please aunty; will you give me one dress tomorrow?"

She looked more polite and obedient.

"Aunty, truly saying, tomorrow is my birthday. I sought money from Papa, genuinely and bought three clothes."

Because of her genuine request, I agreed to give one.

"Okay, come tomorrow at midday." She was very glad.

She began to go out cheerfully. I looked at her figure and began to think. I never saw the joy on my face before any customer. She was about seventeen-eighteen years old daughter of a social activist. I thought she was a college girl and why she didn't have any new dress for three years. She belonged to neither a poor nor very rich family.

The next day, I sewed her one dress. I deliberately sewed it in a new fashion of a three-phase pattern.

Uma came in smiling. She looked more smiling than yesterday. I gave her a dress and water to drink. She went inside and wore the new dress for trial. It was soft silken sky blue embroidered Salwar looking pretty good on her body.

"How was your math paper?"

"Very fine aunty. Certainly, I will get distinction in it," she said.

"Can I look in the mirror?"

She observed her face and Salwar suit in the mirror; she looked very beautiful as if a princess. She laughed fluently.

"It is prepared very fine. I liked it. Wearing this new dress today on my birthday, he will be very glad." she spoke casually.

"Who is he?"

"No, no I mean 'they'"

"Don't conceal anything, Uma, I have never seen any girl so happy in her new dress. Happy Birthday Uma."

She sat on the sofa keeping old clothes in her bag.

"I think you are celebrating your birthday in a grand way. Did you call your friends?"

She was somewhat nervous. Of course, it was our first meeting. I knew her only as a daughter of a social activist.

"No, no, I never celebrate my birthday." She stopped saying. She was conceiting something in mind. I told her that I was like her mother."

"Truly you are like my mother standing in front." She said and began to cry.

"What was happened to cry? If you don't like to say, don't tell, today you are looking in the new dress like a princess. You will look so beautiful when you will become a bride at the wedding."

I took her in empress and consoled her. I prepared tea and served her. She said, "She did not drink tea for four-five years, my mom doesn't allow me to drink tea or milk at home." said Uma.

I was influenced by her behavior while taking tea.

Uma said. "I have no mother. My mother died, when I was a child. My father remarried and I have now a stepmother. My father does not speak to me, because of her rough nature. He behaves like a captive because of her. My home is like a prison for me. I am like a bird kept in a cage whose wings have torn off aspiring to fly. Aunty, would I never get a loving life. My mind is aspiring for love life...."

She was sobbing, shedding tears. I felt sympathy.

"Really, Uma, I had no idea. Why should your mother behave like such? People look at your mother and father with respect. I also think your family is ideal. Sorry, your feelings have been badly affected.

"It is not like it. Everything is not presumed in society. I told you a lie. All things are not true. I told you the father had given money for a dress. But the truth is that that was collected money of my fun food and forcibly given by Bhavik for my birthday. Anybody's mind is searching for love and sympathy. I am one of them."

"Pop had bought a dress for me three years ago. Uncle had given two dresses. I like to live like other collegiate girls. We are not so poor, But Pop neglected me. Mother gives everything to her children's money, books, dresses, toys, etc."

"My stepmother used to beat me for a trivial reason. Now I am somewhat grownup. So she is taunting and scolding me. I do every house chore washing, sweeping and cleaning, etc. except looking." She said.

"Uma, forget everything now, you have cleared twelfth class. Go to another place for further education, you are clever, aspiring. You will find a bright path."

"Yes, your saying is true. I also like to study higher. But my parents are always neglecting me. They have decided to make their children doctors and to teach me B.Sc. But I aim to become a doctor. At the same time, my father is thinking to get me married. I don't think to whom I should share my feelings. Three-four times, I thought of committing suicide. If I had not got that Bhavik, I........"

"Uma, who is Bhavik?"

"He is our neighbor. He loves me very much for two years. He comes to talk to me in alone."

"But do you have a love for him?"

"No, it is not so. I said to him neither yes, nor no. I only here is saying. I do not like it but I find some love and sympathy in his talking."

I observed seriousness in her feelings. She emptied her suppressed feelings before me for the first time.

"Why shouldn't my parents know my feelings? I am wearing the same dress daily and attend college. I received a fifth of dress from Bhavik for the first time and it is also because of his obstinate nature. When I refused to accept it, she threatened me to commit suicide. Once Bhavik consumed poison thinking that I was avoiding him. He behaves like a mad. He loves youth. I like him. But I cannot accept or refuse him for marriage because of family conditions. He has a government job of fifteen thousand rupees. His parents have jobs, a good house, and a car. He is the only son of his parents. One day, he warned me to marry him otherwise he would commit suicide. I am feared and confused. He also warned my parents that he would not allow anybody to marry her. He wanders around my home and college to have my look."

"What should I do, Aunty, will I get anyway? Should I elope with him? But his house is near ours. So where we will live. One thing I forget to tell you, the difference between our ages is of seventeen years. He is too much elder. I fear this distance of age in practical life. He touched me once against my will. But sometimes I feel to embrace him, kiss him and obtain love from him which I am deprived of my parents. My mind is in a complex situation. Sometimes I think my affair will blacken the reputation of my parent. I think my parents will not spend too much money on my marriage. Bhavik will also get and very good girl But my mind is entangled in him."

Uma told me everything clearly and openly like a C.D. player.

I said, "Dear, Uma, your problem and question are complicated. Think widely and wisely and decide for yourself up to your future. You have to mold your career. Future education, harassment of your stepmother, willful nature of Bhavik, higher difference in your age, whether to marry or leave Bhavik, etc. questions have made your life complicated and like a prison."

Her birthday is never celebrated. Stepmother celebrates the birthday of her children.

"Aunty, I celebrate my birthday in mind only in a new dress. They do not allow me to participate. Dad also celebrated his fifteenth birthday. I am thinking of all these things on the terrace. I cannot blame anybody, my fate is false. I do not believe in fate, luck, future etc. The difference is increasing between me and my parents, Bhavik, and life; sometimes I think this distance will decrease after my death. At the same time, I think about why I should commit suicide. I have to live. I have to come over all these circumstances."

By hearing her life story, I was overwhelmed. She emptied her feeling with a heavy heart. She would be feeling fresh. She was looking like a princess in her new dress. Fresh attractive and beautiful. She took the bag of her old clothes and said goodbye to me and began to go out. I was looking at her again and again thinking something missing forever.

I began to sew the clothes. The 'Tik... tik... tik... tik....' of sawing machine, the wheel was going on reminding me of the pathetic life story of Uma.

I slept very late at night. I awoke early with a headache. I sprinkled face paper vendor dropped a newspaper at the door. I took the paper and began to read the district page. I came across headline news. I began to fall unconscious. My husband who was in bed asked me, "what is happening and fell." My husband lifted me and ask, 'what has happened?' I came to consciousness. I was thinking of yesterday's incidents, "Aunty, may I come in?" I saw a half sewed dress on the machine; again darkness prevailed before my eyes. I was faint. My husband was saying to me, "Wake up..... Wake up...."

Social worker Salve's daughter committed suicide,
Uma salve suicide.....
Suicide reason unknown..........
The investigation is going..............

VII
Local

A path from the black stone tunnel was going towards the smooth flow of the Narmada River. My daily routine was to hold hands to pay Shambhu located on a greenery-covered hill.

A wide body of the River Narmada, green beautiful rush railway route at the left side of the village producing harsh sound tour during mind. So teat path was the only solace to the mind.

I had just passed nineteen years in this village. But my acute poverty of eighteen universes had not exhausted. I sat near the trunk of the Pipal tree, lifted a pebble, and threw in the water of Narmada Ripples becoming wider reached my heart and mingled.

sala, the mind is always disturbed by thoughts. An empty mind is always a devil's workshop. Some there are lingering in an empty mind in isolation. But after hearing the harsh whiling sound of the local train at seven in the evening, my mind also began to jump.

That day I traveled by the local train. Was a heavy rush of passengers? A railway journey is cheaper than buses and so everybody is to travel by train.

Traveling by train once in three-four months is refreshing mind. Most of the passengers in local are poverty-ridden in rags.

My mind is as if running hither and thither. So I spend most of the time sitting on the bank of Narmada and observing the calm, still water, Quiet and cold, Sacred Narmada. But when I go home, Narmada in my house is quite quarrelsome women. She is always complaining. this is exhausted and that is not in the house. go and bring and don't tell about children.... always shouting and demanding fifteen years passed of my marriage.

Only regret and regret. Aare Ho! It would have been better if I had been better if. I had been a bachelor like that Madhukar. How fine and enjoying the life he has!

Luck of anyone. Oh no, man is the master of his fate. He had decided to get married. But I was eager to get married earlier.

For what is marriage necessary? family happiness or anything else! Lust..... No, no, It is better not to think of it. So if bachelorhood is enough? Why is the money of happiness needed? But anybody should of love and affection to talk to a accompany.

But this brat my wife. After marriage, she is having loved like a new bride with for two years. After the birth of children, everything disappeared.

What to say about women. They even dislike washing clothes, cleaning utensils, and looking. Aare ho, what can I say about to days meals. No test at all. Only boiled in oil, water, salt, or chili powder. comparatively, Madhukar's life was better. How can Madhukar enjoy with people! "Flies are fluttering around sweets." He has turned to be a half politician. presidents of societies run after him.

How many days passed! I have been thinking of committing suicide, but don't dare. But anyway I will have to. How long should I survive! Otherwise, people will murder me. I am passing my days only in thinking. What will happen to me? My life is like of ants and insects Service. That is also of a High school teacher. What benefit?

Dark clouds were crowding in the sky. Darkness was to prevail. Now the local train will arrive in a moment.

I heard the fluttering sound by the flow of the water. Who would be? Animal, bird, Who will be coming? Who likes such isolated life? Only me I like.... How a dead man is taking sound sleep silently in a grave! He is like a Saint or Mahant.

On the right side near the bush, something went crawling inside the mound.

Let's see! Oh, it is a hare. Should I catch it? We see hares many times. The hunters catch them and sell each for thirty-forty rupees. It is said, the soup is very tasty. I have not enjoyed its taste these days. I have not enjoyed mutton's test for six months.

Ha! That day, Dadu was asking for mutton. I assured him to bring it on coming Sunday. Today is Sunday, what a co-incident. Aare Ha! Where did it go that hare? Should I catch it? But I have never eaten its meat. But children will feel it better. Let's try to catch it. If will run away from this Mound. But I have a kerchief to catch.

I looked around. It was time to darken. The local was late that day. The Narmada was quite calm. I looked at it in the round. It was very lovable. I dropped kerchief on its body and caught it once. It was trying to escape from my hands. Its eyes were very beautiful. It was as soft and lovable as cotton.

It was stretching, trying to escape. Will it run away? Should I kill it? It will be easier to carry. I took a sharp-edged black stone and killed the <u>haje</u> with it like a criminal.

But what can I say? My mind was full of tears. I was shuddering. Yes, I have murdered the hare. I was thinking of myself committing suicide. But to its contrary, I have killed the hare. Nobody should know about it. Otherwise, the foresters will arrest me. The small head of the hare was dancing in my mind; frightening me.

My legs were crossing the rough path towards the village swiftly. The dead hare was in the handkerchief beetles started crying. It was about seven p.m. The local arrived late whistling. The street lamp's on the poles were on. my wife would be preparing for cooking. I should go early.

Dadu and Rani took a knife and pot went by the side of the bathroom and cut the flesh of the hare. My wife would have been pleased. But seeing the read pieces of meat, I felt hatred.

Aaha! But no vegetable oil for cooking. My wife had told me in the morning. 'The grocery was exhausted.' The payment was back for six months. Will the shopkeeper give grocery on credit again?

I took a bag. I thought I would promise the shopkeeper to pay his amount as soon as he receives his salary. He agreed and gave me groceries.

Sala, the mutton soup was very tasty. Dadu and Rani had eaten plenty and slept. We both husband and wife started our meals. It was about three-fourth kilo mutton. I had an opportunity of eating mutton after six months and so the taste was different. My wife was delighted but I was depressed 'killed.' Yes, I have killed.

My wife urged me to buy a Saree after payment. She has ornaments, new dresses, new Sarees, etc. But no value to husband; bought only one dress in four years. I have also some desires and liking but who will think. Father expired leaving a debt of lakh rupees. to get only seven thousand. three-four thousand for debt and interest amount and two thousand in other deductions. what remains for grocery, house rent, the electric bill, house expenditure.

Sala, The president of the school society had demanded the amount for the school building construction. The donations were paid earlier. Gone is the age of honesty of Gandhiji Baba. No way to complain. Because of private school. School is private property to despite receiving grants; the president demands teachers' salaries.

We have to pay. To whom should we say? It is like, "hidden treasure in a mist." It will be better if the president of the school will die. Nobody tortures us like. He turned seventy-one years and celebrated his birthday on the money of the teachers.

He abused the teachers, spends day and night in school. His house in front of the school never talks politely with teachers. Everybody took dinner. My wife slept. But because of the tension, I have the habit of late-night sleep.

That hare was running. I was following it. Caught to beat with a stone. You have killed me. I will not let you go. Murdered me.

The ghost of the hare was torturing me. I could not sleep. It was a dream. I was carrying to save me. Breathed last. My wife, Dadu, Rani are crying for me. Who will look after them? They will be. Nothing was left for them. My wife was carrying. The neighbors say's "Wipe of Kunku....."

Why would she cry? Never understood me with love. Whether she could love me? parents, wife, and children nobody understood my feelings. Always quarreling. Once she complained of me in the police station also. Quarrel today; take dinner on one plate tomorrow.

That sound of the local train. Suicide, no those four-five ghost of problems coming towards me. That shopkeeper, debt's of the bank that hares, etc. But after death, who will pay the debts.

That Damodhar was also engrossed by the ghost on the tamarind tree. He became mentally disturbed and died.

Alas! Therefore I didn't go that deep flow of the Narmada. Five people drowned there and their ghosts are wandering. I don't believe it.

Oh! I would be saved from the clutches of the President of society. But what to him. He will be benefitted. Another teacher would be appointed in my place. He will pay lakhs of donation to the resident. He will laugh.

Freed from the family circus. Nobody is tired to understand me. My only isolated and lonely life, all disappeared.

That bachelor Madhukar ...... I....my Narmada....Dadu...., Rani.... crying. family members, relatives well-wishers all assembled.

Yes, the messenger of death.....hanged.... those crossed ropes around the neck.... will kill....... now will pull...... last breath .... last..... truth.

I bade farwell to all. Meet if retorn. Otherwise the life of cats and dogs.... birth ....no.... no....

Laughed that God of death laughed tremendously. Pulled the rope and pushed all of sudden..... the end.

I heard a sudden loud sound. I woke up. It was six in the morning. I am alive. I didn't believe it. Every day was well, wife, Dadu, Rani It was only a dream.

Today a cup of tea in front in the morning and without demanding. What a pleasant surprise!

She smiled and I stared at her.

"Dear, your founder president expired."

"My sip of tea sprinkled out of the mouth.

"What?" I said.

"Yes, he had gone for morning walk at five a.m. He was crushed under the train while crossing the route as he could not see the train, it is said." She said.

"The whole village is going towards the accident place to see."

I started at the hill through the windows. Again I saw the ghost of the hare wandering in the fresh clear sky.

The local train of half-past six of morning..... Sound of Whistle. I put on the clothes and began to go towards the local.

VIII
Surkuda

Tukaram took Surkuda in his hand, filled a bundle of leaves of dates updates at one in Surkuda, and carrying it on one shoulder began to go to the field in torn clothes. His wife Rakhma was also carrying a basket containing Shidori. (packet of bhakaris)

Tukaram looked at the sky. It was full of dark clouds in the month of Margshish. Paddy crop was lying cut in the fields. It would be collected and shaped in a heap after two to three days. But because of the fear of untimely rains, Tukaram had to collect it; otherwise, it would be washed out and destroyed.

Tukaram had got a share of two acres of land in brotherhood and the life of his all family members was depending on it. He had two daughters. No profit has gained in paddy cultivation. If it's feeding, It is enough. He had his younger brother Madhav. He was clever. Their father thought to teach him and he was admitted to the village school. After studying seventh class, He went to a town for further education. We afforded him for his higher education by hook or Creole. He stayed in a hostel and passed B.Com. Exam. He got a job as a clerk and was later promoted to a Saheb. He got married to a city girl and had two sons. All these happened after our father's death. Twelve years after marriage, the attitude of Madhav was completely changed. Before getting a job, he had sympathy for brothers and sister-in-law. But his city wife had changed his behavior. They used to come to our village occasionally and would stay only for a night. She could not like our village hut-type house smeared with cow dung. She could not like our cattle shade, smoking Chulha (fireplace), and dirty surrounding. One day, They came to stay for four days but she disliked our poor rustic life and went city after a day.

Once Tukaram had to go with his family to Madhav in a city, however stayed they for one night. But she disliked Tukaram's family members. Without giving any guest attitude, she sent them back to the village. Sometimes Tukaram's two daughters willfully asked to go to their uncle's house but in vain.

Real brotherhood was not left in educated Madhav, He had demanded his share of land five years back. Only four acres of land were distributed among the two brothers. Tukaram learn that day that only educated employed men can exploit uneducated persons. But there was no solution.

That day Madhav had come to our Village. Rakhma becomes very glad. She was preparing kandhe Bhaje. Both the brother was sitting on a cot. both the daughter was busy in their study.

"Dada, I came for one work." Madhav Said hesitatingly. Tukaram sensed something wrong would happen.

"What is the work? Why do you shame?"

"Nothing else. you will be angry. But I have no solution. I have decided to build a house."

Tukaram became glad in a moment. He thought his brother would build a house in a central place in the village. He would have to live in a cement building.

"What is there to ask? Build it. I cannot say you no." Tukaram said.

"But Dada, you know, a plot of land in a city is very costly and how can one build a cement concrete house," said Madhav.

Tukaram's face darkens.

"Dada, I have to sell my share of two acres of land," said Madhav. Tukaram reminded silent. Tears began rolling down from his eyes. They were taking dinner. Nobody talked. Dinner had no taste. Madhav was employed in a city landing luxurious life. It was better for him to give that land to his poor village brother morally. On the contrary, he was demanding a piece of land. Tukaram was paying for Madhav's education also after their father's death.

Madhav went to the city in the morning. He had sold his two acres of land. Tukaram was depressed. He was thinking of his daughter's education, their marriage, and future life. If Madhav had co-operated, Tukaram's daughters would be taught in a city. They were deprived of uncle's love and sympathy.

Talking together, Tukaram and his wife reached their field. The sky was full of clouds and it would rain anytime. They were in a hurry to make a heap of cut paddy crop. Tukaram spread one end of the Surkuda in the earth. Both began to tie bundles of the crying crops. If it rained, it would destroy the whole crop and it was not affordable. Some twenty-thirty sacks of paddy would be destroyed.

Madhav had built a building in the City. Five rooms, marble tiles, wall-compound, etc. like a bungalow. Tukaram and his family had gone for house warming ceremony but because of Madhav's wife, they had to return village the next day. To find selfishness and forget Tukaram was in his behaviors.

After six months, Madhav came to the village on the occasion of Diwali. Our daughters began to dance seeing their uncle. But he did not pamper them. After coming from the field, Tukaram asked him, "How did you come? Is everything right?"

"Yes, everything is ok. But I came here for some work?"

"What has left again?"

"Dada, I have to sell them half shares of this house," said Madhav.

Tukaram became furious,

"Despite having a new building, you are demanding your half share of this hut type's house in the village. What have we not done for you? Take it, take it and do what you have to do."

Tears rolled down from his eyes. A cup of tea and broke from Rakhma's hand. Her hands were shuddering. Pin-drop silence spread. Nobody talked. Madhav went out. Tukaram was waiting for lunch but he had left for his city never to come to the village.

Tukaram thought his brother was behaving like an enemy. He had forgotten every sacrifice done by Tukaram. He had done by Tukaram. He had none but his wife and two daughters.

Both wife and husband looked at the cloudy and stormy sky and prayed God of Rains not to pour down until a heap of bundles of the crop was completed. They tide the bundles of the crop in hurry. Tukaram was entangling the two bundles at the two ends of the Surkuda keeping on the shoulders. He was making a round shape heap of the bundles of paddy crop. Rakhma was helping him in lifting the bundles. The clouds very moving swiftly. The strong wind was blowing with thundering rakhma was giving the bundles and Tukaram was making the heap in round shape. At last, the round shape heap of paddy crop was made and they took a deep sigh.

Tukaram and his wife were returning home with long strides as daughters were waiting at home. Lightning flashed in a moment and it began to rain. Rakhama entered the home. Tukaram kept the Surkuda straight in the courtyard. He looked at both the Bullocks who were kept under the tamarind tree. He went there and untied. Both the bullocks ran into the shed. In the meantime, The lightning flashed with thunder.

Without knowing anything, all of a sudden, the lightning fell on the tamarind tree in which Tukaram fell unconscious on the ground never to wake up. Everything happened in a moment, flash of lighting, running of bullocks for shelter, heavy showering, and Tukaram's death.

Two daughters rushed to him crying, "My master." They began crying. Hearing the Cries, the neighbors assembled around Tukaram in the stormy rains.

Rains, storms, lightning everything was silent after an hour. Evening darkness was about to spread. The news of Tukaram death due to a lightning strike spread all over.... The noise of the crying, assembling of people, Police Patil..... Sarpanch.... Police panchnama..... Investigation.....

Madhav knew the news and he came with his city wife in the morning. Rakhma and her daughter were crying throughout the night. Tukaram had not eaten anything. They lost their man support. The neighbor put the wood in the bullock cart for cremation.

"Aare, Yeru Ghya Yeru... Chala Tiradi Bandhuya. Take a Bamboo to prepare a Tirdi," Somebody said,

"There was no Bamboo in Tukaram house. The search was on."

Lastly, Surkuda was found. Madhav took Surkuda,

"Take This Bamboo Surkuda and cut it into pieces to build Tiradi. Now was of no use."

"It was done so. kept on Tiradi."

Tukaram's dead body was bathed, clothes were covered, and was worshipped. Crying was on and Madhav also shed tears. Rukhma and his daughter touched his feet in crying. Rukhma's....... and Bangals were broken. the gold bead was kept in Tukaram mouth, The whole village assembled for the funeral procession.

"Ha, lift the Thirdi, "four relatives lifted Tirdi on which Tukaram's dead body was lying. Funeral procession of Tukaram dead body started. Madhav took axe and sup and was walking ahead of Tirdi. Bullock cart carrying wood was ahead and then Dafara was beaten. Tukaram used to carry Surkuda on his shoulders for taking crop bundles. That surkuda was now carrying the dead body of Tukaram to the crematory. Surkuda was the loan companion of Tukaram. What apathetic!

IX

Inda

Ganpya's marriage took place in a grand way. His wife was also beautiful. What is more, needed from a person having two acres of land and doing wages?

At the time of the marriage procession, Chandrakala was sitting in the bullock cart. But she was looking more beautiful than the moon. Ganpya was very pleased to get the bride from a neighborly village. A dowry system in Sav Teli community. Her father was too poor. So he married his daughter in the Yendile Teli community. What her father was to do! "Garibala Gat Nahi Aani Kuni Bhik Det Nahi" donation is not given to a poor man. Her father became poor because of his five daughters' marriages.

Chandri was beautiful as well as a hard-working girl making a diamond of dust. She used to sell the bundles of sticks. She was strong and stout, her round-shaped face was beautiful and attractive. And so police Patil's son caught her hand in the field of Tur and tried to molest her. If she had cried loudly, What would have happened. She became an adolescent and her father got her married to Ganpya. Her father was poor otherwise she would have got to reach her husband.

After marriage procession bride and groom came. Chandri was sad to see Ganpya's house but what she was to do on her first honeymoon night, was somewhat nervous. Ganpaya sat near her and took her hand. Patil's son had caught her hand but it was a different thing. Now she had romantic emotions. Her long-cherished fragrant flower-like adolescent was crushed in the first night. Everything was calm.

To get early, complete the house chores and go to daily wages in the fields was the daily routine. Ganpya had two acres of land and it had enough grains to earn the livelihood of his family. They had nobody's debt, not anything.

The rainy season started. Cultivations of the field need more labor. Ganpya and Chandri used to go to Patile's fields for daily wages of twenty rupees. Some ten to twelve laborers work daily in the Patil's farm. Now Chandri was familiar to everybody as usual they were working in the field. The strong wind broke out with light showers of rain. The lightning was flashing with thunder in the sky. The cultivating work was stopped. All the workers entered the farm hut. Women's started gossiping. Chandri was frightened and did not speak anything.

The lighting flashed on the brass water vessel.

"We have never seen such a continuous flash of lighting."

"And if anybody is Inda, lighting flash has liked this."

"But nobody is Inda in our village."

"It is saying- Inda majha Bal Aani Jiwala Kal."

"If anybody Inda among us?"

"If anybody is, please go to your house early."

Women were talking together. Chandri was new and a new bridge among them. Though she was frightened, she was laughing. She could know what is happening. After

Two-Three hours all the workers returned home hurriedly.

At night Chandra was Busy in thinking. Without enjoying romantic movement on the bed with Ganpya, She was, again and again, thinking of the lightning. She was tired of day work also and slept.

Chandra was thinking all the time of the lightning. She could not understand the meaning of Inda and its relations with lightening. All women were frightened. I was also frightened but why I was smiling in mind in that terrible frightening atmosphere I was smiling. Perhaps I would be Inda. But what is Inda? How does it happen? Whom should I ask? All these questions were unanswered because I had no mother-in-law to ask. I cannot ask other women.

Then came the first festival "Aakhadi" She had come to her mother's home for the celebrations of the first Aakhadi. All her four sisters were at their husband's houses.

"Ma, buy me a silken saree like other sisters."

"You are working in farmland and stay at home. So why do you want a silk saree?" Ma said.

"No, I want a silk saree," Chandra said.

Lastly, the mother agreed to buy her silk saree. On the first Diwali festival, she would have to buy a saree for Chandra and a dress for her husband.

Chandri and her mother took dinner and they were talking late at night. Her father was asleep. Chandri now thought to ask her mother about Inda.

"Ma, What is Inda?" Chandra's question disrupted his mother's mood.

"Ha, Inda is there, but I don't know. Why do you ask me?"

"No, that day we were working in the field. the lightning was striking. women were saying, Inda Majha bal, Jiwala Kal." Inda person is a danger to other's life in lightening.

Mother began to sob. "Why are you crying, Ma? Chandra asked.

"Daughter doesn't go out in lightning. You will be the reason for other's death."

Chandri asked her mother, "if she was Inda?"

"Yes, yes, the daughter you are Inda. You were born Inda."

"But Ma, what is Inda? How is Inda born?"

"Yes, now I tell you everything. But the daughter doesn't tell anybody. swear it. You would know the story of the "Mahabharata" Wasudeo and Devaki had given birth a daughter. Her uncle Kansa lifted that girl and moved around and around angrily to kill her. But she slipped from his hand and went to the sky and became lightning. She was Inda. it is said from that time lightening is frightened of Inda person. Pori, when you were born, I feared your broken fate.

I did not tell to anybody. You are Inda and so the lightning does not fall on you. When it flashes, you are laughing and it falls on others. So at such time, you should not stay with them. You should leave the place and go home alone. Why you should endanger others' life.

Ma wiped off tears and told everything at a stroke.

Chandri heard everything silently and began to weep to blame her fate. "But Ma, how I was born Inda and how can I be known as Inda?"

"Pori, listen. Your elder sister Shilpa was born before earlier to you. I had not discharged monthly period after her birth and I conceived you." Ma began to weep.

"Whether it is boy or girl, it is called Inda." Both began to weep.

"lightening will strike anybody anywhere and I will be blamed." thought Chandra. Both slept in thinking.

Chandri stayed four-five days in her mother's house. She was given a new silk saree and her father sent her to her husband's house accompanying her.

Chandri and Ganpya were engaged in their marriage life. The rainy season started. Paddy plants were grown five-six inches long. Farmer started the work of transplanting the paddy plant. Chandri and Ganpat used to go to fieldwork to see the clear sky. Chandri hesitated to tell Ganpya of Inda.

Today transplanting of paddy started in their field. Ten-twelve women were busy transplanting. Ganpya was plowing the field in mud. At midday, the sky was full of dark clouds. Rain drizzles began to shower lightning started flashing.

Chandri looked at the sky. She was frightened as well as smiling in mind. She thought to return home but doubted women would ask her. All the women covered their heads with branches of Paras tree.

"Ye, Chandri, Dhar Na V Dokshyavar Dhar" Put a branch on the head. "Parsacche Daravani Angavar Vij Nahi Padat." Because of the paras branch lightning does not strike on the head.

Chandri had no attention to women's suggestions. She was busy thinking. Lightening was flashing before her legs. All the women were frightened. The transplanting work was stopped and all the women were standing in the shed. They thought it was better to save a life than the work.

Chandri took a branch of Paras tree on her head. She was looking at the sky ample praying, "Oh God, don't have any calamity on others because of me!" She began to laugh. All women were looking at her and know that she was Inda. Ganpya kept looking at Chandra. Her whole body became wet due to rainwater. She looked like a fairy in heaven in the flash of lightning. Ganpya was staring at her beautiful shining face.

Chandri began to go back home speedily. Women were gossiping. Ganpya was also frightened. He was looking at her back figure. It was raining heavily with lightning and thunder. After half an hour everything was silent. The fields were full of rainwater. Some drops were making ripples on-field water. "Inda......"

X

Sonzari

('Sonzari' means a person who collects particles of gold from the ash in the shop of Goldsmith.)

I am cast by Sonzari. The last fortnight of the summer started. The heat of the searching sun-like burns. the sunset was falling from the body like water.

Fifty years passed after the country's freedom. But the poor cannot get to times meal, the cold wind of fan or cooler is far away. Gone are the white British but the black ones are created. People are saying of a computer but the poor have not simple fan or T.V. in their huts. They are leading a life with "Bhakar and Choon."

We have the habit to work in any season. Now the Mriga be Nakshatra started still the sun is scorching. I knew that the mother of Dago Divanji secretary expired. As soon as I heard, the news, I asked the neighbour when will the cremation of Aaji take place.

The cremation was at midday and the remains will be emersed tomorrow in the Markanda River. It was my profession also to find collect some gold particles from the ashes of the dead. We earn something from it.

I told my wife Laxmi, she felt well. She used to do some work in the fields. We came to live in this village five years ago. We built a small hut here. Before that, we were wandering from village to village. As per our caste of Sonzari, Our ancestors had also to wander from place to place and lead life.

It was not a bad profession so far. Is the gold lying on road? In the past, the goldsmith used to make ornaments of gold, silver, copper, etc. We used to find some particles are gold, silver, etc. from the ashes and we used to sell that collected gold! But it took too much labor. Nowadays the ornaments are made on machines without burning coal or ashes.

My wife Laxmi and I used to go to the big in the shapes of the goldsmith with a broom, brush, and open spread mouth pot.(Ghamela) We used to by the ashes of his Bhatti of heating metal. We used to go to the well or river to wash ashes and separate my particles from sand or ashes. I find some particles of gold we used to sell them and earn a livelihood. We had two starve many times. Children used to beg for food in the village.

Now a day we have almost stopped our ancestral profession and led a life of doing field works. But occasionally we do our profession somebody died and after is the time it's ashes emersion. Each village has one or two cast houses. It is the olden tradition that one or two beads are kept in the mouth of the dead man are some ornament on the dead body of women and cremated in fire. We use to collect the ashes of a dead body and wash it, clean it, and try to find some particles of gold.

"Ba, will you buy me a new dress when school starts?" asked my younger son Bhisanya. He was learning in the fourth class. My elder son Raman was learning in twelfth class.

"Ha, I will buy you a new dress, slate, pencil next time when you when I go to market." My son became glad, ate something more, and slept. My both sons are clever.

I am a thumb printer illiterate, master used to tell me to teach my son. He admitted Raman to a hostel in a town. Raman is simple like me. He will pass the twelfth class. I pray he will at least get a job of peon.

My wife Laxmi reminded me to go to Sonzari. I set up in the early morning. Raman was to go to school to see the results. Patil had told about the resulting news. It will be better if his lad passes the twelfth exam. But it is not so easy. Thinking so, I reached the crematory. relatives of the deceased had collected the remaining unburned bones of the deceased and were going to the Markhanda Rivers for emission. I was looking standing for away. All the relatives of Dago Divanji were returning home. some were sobbing.

Dago Divanji was a rich man so I thought I would get some gold. I went near that place of burning and collected the ashes in a big bag. I began to wash it in the flow of the river water.

"Who is there and what is doing?" a cowboy asked.

"I am Sonzari, Ji. Washing ashes."

"Did you find something?"

"No, just started washing," I said.

Feeding his cattle with river water, he went out. I was hungry. I untied a Gathodi (packing) of Bhakaris began to eat. I found there three-four packages of Chivada under the tree. I tasted Chivada. It was tasty. I found that Chivada packages in one end of my Dupatta. My sons will enjoy it.

After eating bread with raw onion, I began I wash the ashes. the sun was scorching. My waist was aching. The whole ashes were to be washed soon. But I did not find anything. The relatives are greedy; they search if anything left and take it out. I was nervous. I thought my labor was proving fruitless.

I was washing the ashes in the Ghamela in water and moving my palms swiftly over it. In the meantime, fortunately, I found a silver ring in the ashes weighing about two Todas (20 grams) I was very glad. I thought I would get at least four hundred rupees. I was washing the ashes of the last Ghamela. There was nothing. I was about to throw it in the water. I saw somewhat glittering yellowish. It was a gold piece weighing about one Toda. I took it on palm and began to observe it for a long time miraculously. I packed Ghamela, broom, brush, etc. Wash hand and began to go home.

Laxmi will be very pleased. Bisaya will get new school dresses. some money will be at my disposal. Five-six months Raman would be gone to school to see exam results. If he passed the exam, I will after coconut and sweet to Goddess Ganga Mata. Raman will get new dresses. He earns four-five rupees by distributing the newspaper. The sun was setting. I reached home. I was keeping my washing materials. I saw a master coming.

"What does your Raman says? Today the result is declared." He said. "Raman did not come yet. We didn't know if he passed."

Master sat on the rope cot. Laxmi began to boil tea.

"Why are you preparing tea? I came to tell you to distribute Jalebi. Raman stood first in the school." As soon as the master declared, I was shocked and surprised.

I asked, "How did you know about Raman's result, Guruji?"

"Are, I had gone to taluka. I met Raman there, he will come tomorrow. I sent him there to the secretary for a job in the bank. I talked to the secretary." He said. I began to dream. I will pay the debt. My joys knew no bounds.

I came home and told Laxmi everything. She also becomes very glad. At night, I was thinking Raman and slept.

I got up early. Laxmi told me that Sadu Mang died at night. I was shocked. We talked yesterday. He said that 'he had to go to son's village.' He led horrible hard life by dragging the dead animals. Has son got a job of peon? Before enjoying some happy life with his son, he died.

My son Raman will also get a job. My life will be changed but I fear I will also die like Sadu Mang. all of a sudden. My ashes will also be washed out to search for some gold particles.

I came from the crematory rituals of Sadu Mang. Raman came from the town. He got the job of a clerk in a bank. We all were very happy because of the blessing up goddess Ganga maa.

I heard "Will you come tomorrow for Sonzari?" It was Namabhau coming to me. I was remembering the dead body of Sadu Mang in my eyes. I was thinking of my dead body lying near his..........

www.ingramcontent.com/pod-product-compliance
Lightning Source LLC
Chambersburg PA
CBHW061337120726
48001CB00002B/911